THIRD ACT DATING

A GUIDE TO COMPANIONSHIP FOR SILVER SINGLES

by Gillian Royes, Ph.D.

For those who haven't given up.

I've created an online course that takes seniors looking for companionship through the dating process. It's a step-by-step guide that answers all the questions that I've heard while teaching older folks how to expand their social circle, including by dating. The course features videos and downloadable resources to enhance the learning experience, making it easy to understand and implement in daily life. The twelve episodes in the course cover a range of topics including preparing yourself for the dating process, finding ways to expand your social circle, and even putting up an online profile safely, if that's the route you choose. My goal is to give you all the tools you'll need to find new companions and enhance your lifestyle.

For more information visit www.ThirdActDating.com

Table of Contents

Preface

I was overjoyed to find love late in life. My new partner and I were both creatives working from home and enjoyed exploring museums and traveling. As we were in the throes of planning to marry, he got ill and, since we were both expecting him to recover, his death came as a shock. After the paramedics and funeral staff had gone, after the quiet service and departure of loved ones, my grief ebbed, flowed, and eventually subsided. Finding myself alone, questions arose: How do I restructure my life? Do I remain alone forever or risk looking for love again?

This last conundrum was new to me. In the 30 years of being single before, romance had always been around the corner, always different. It became a practical issue for me and my single friends. Two people can live cheaper than one, we agreed, and better to live with someone in case of, well, anything. We changed with the times, with the internet and senior dating websites. We went on dates and kissed more than a few frogs. Some liaisons ended in commitment, some in disappointment, a few in disaster. But the hope was always there that the next frog would turn out to be the prince or princess with whom we'd live happily forever.

What I discovered when I lived with my partner was that long term relationships are *hard*, harder after grooves of behaviors and attitudes have been established. Social habits, political leanings, spiritual beliefs, food choices, not to mention sexual wants or the lack of them, are different for everyone. Just sleeping together could be frustrating if one mate reads in bed late or another one snores. Staying in a relationship takes flexibility and adaptation.

My parents had mastered the art of remaining together through thick and thin. After my father died, my mother lived for eighteen lonely, depressed years, comparing every passing man to her husband. Her sad end has been a lesson for me. So when, after my partner died, my daughter commented that being single could take me on an upward trajectory, not a downward one, it was an Aha moment for me. I was now free to do and be whatever I wanted. She made me think, as your children often do, about a new future. I went back to my writing, although not novels as I had previously done.

I started writing about being alone. It was so depressing, however, that I decided to go another route. I already had a podcast called *Third Act Dating,* so I began working on this book as an expansion of that podcast, exploring the options open to senior singles for romantic relationships, including not having one. While writing the book, I was invited to teach a course on dating to seniors, a class which proved more popular than I'd imagined and expanded to several courses at different institutions, which have been satisfying, fun and thought-provoking.

I began to realize that I was uniquely positioned to teach the classes and write this book. Although I am neither a therapist nor a medical doctor, I have a Ph.D. in Communication and Social History from Emory University and taught interpersonal communication at two universities for over 20 years. I was also lead writer of a book called *Sexcess: The New Gender Rules at Work* about communication between men and women.

Most importantly, I have lots of personal experience since I've been single and dating for the last 30 years. Two of my online relationships had been long-term, including the last, tragically interrupted one. Because of my success with dating, I kept getting requests from friends about how they too could succeed in the dating game, which was the origin of the podcast.

This book is for those who find themselves without a mate in their latter years and are considering seeking one. Whether you've been alone for a long time, divorced or recently lost your partner, there is no shame in seeking companionship. The chapters are meant to provide you with the pros and cons, dos and don'ts, my personal experiences, and enough information to help you make decisions along the way. The facts that I include are from articles about research by reputable organizations conducted within five years of the book's publication, unless otherwise stated.

I even include a chapter on living options for those who ultimately decide not to date. The checklists at the end of each chapter are meant to clarify your thoughts about the ideas you've just read about. Looking deep within and answering honestly will help you make the choices that feel right for you.

Read, think and choose wisely, my single friend. Your happiness awaits.

Chapter One
Making A Fresh Start

A fter the passing of my fiancé, I moved to a nearby city where I knew no one. My thinking was that, with the ocean nearby, I would grieve and heal faster. Every afternoon I would take long walks along the beach or by the riverwalk, observing my new town, and I would pass other seniors, all of whom appeared coupled off. It seemed to me that all the other over-65s were happily in relationship. Except me.

Discovering the Reality

Before I allowed myself to get maudlin and sad, I resorted to the internet, my go-to place, to find out how accurate my assumption was. I was surprised to find that I was definitely not alone.

A Pew Research Institute study found that half of all women in the US over 65 were single in 2020. Unfortunately, only 21 percent of men over 65 are single, Pew found, thanks to men marrying later and dying younger than women.

Twenty-one percent to 50 percent? That was more than twice as many single women than men over 65. The odds for single senior women were pretty daunting. Suddenly, the hand-holding by older couples, which seemed so sweet at first, made sense. The woman was making sure everyone knew he was taken.

It became clear that if I as a senior female was going to date, I'd have to build up my courage, be a risk taker again. But I was hardly ready.

Grieving

After being a homebound caregiver for the last months of my partner's life, I found myself now with unlimited time on my hands, surfing the internet, napping, playing solitaire and taking hot baths. But I felt guilty all the way, having been an industrious entrepreneur, writer and lecturer for most of my adult life. I finally accepted that I was grieving, that I needed to go fully through the process if I was ever going to socialize again.

There's grief with every death, divorce or separation, just as there is to a lesser extent with the loss of a pet, a home or a job. Some people defer grieving by throwing themselves into a frenzy of work, gardening, cooking, drinking, doing drugs, anything to forget the loss. But grieve we should.

I discovered this quote from the University of Washington's Counseling Center:

2

Grieving… is important because it allows us to 'free-up' energy that is bound to the lost person, object, or experience—so that we might re-invest that energy elsewhere.

Until we grieve effectively, we are likely to find reinvesting difficult; a part of us remains tied to the past.

After reading this, I decided that I had to work hard at grieving if I was going to free up energy and make space for newer things in my life.

I allowed myself to remember the nurturing, happy times as well as the not-so-fun times and found comfort in everyday occurrences. When the orchid my partner had struggled to revive bloomed, I took it as a sign that he was letting me know he was still around. When I found his walking cane lying on the closet floor after I'd put it away, I was sure he was thanking me for handing it to him just before the stroke took him away. As the weeks went on, I gradually got back to a more normal schedule. When I sometimes lapsed back into my former apathy, I'd go to the public library and choose a new book, or go for a walk to shift my mood.

Whether one has spiritual beliefs or not, it's appropriate and necessary to allow ourselves to grieve. It's a human response to loss. Stopping the grieving process prevents us from moving on successfully to the next stage of life.

When a senior finds him or herself single again, many emotions surface in reaction to the loss of a loved one. It's important for us to be honest about those feelings, be they anger, sadness, shock, relief, guilt, pain or resentment. And it's important to be able to express these feelings. Trying to handle your lingering gloom or sadness on your own can mean that negative emotions hang around for a much longer time.

Grieving can even become a habit that the griever doesn't want to let go of. I had a friend who, up to two years after his wife died, used to curl up in the fetal position on his bed for hours a day until his new girlfriend put a stop to it.

When unhappy emotions won't go away, you might need the help of a therapist or clergy member. Thank goodness, I was able to go through the negative emotions and come out the other side.

Venturing Out

Since the few people I knew in the city I had moved to were busy, I spent almost every day alone. After I woke up one morning with my arms wrapped around my torso, I knew it was time to connect with others. My quiet apartment had become my comfort zone, but chatting to the supermarket cashier wasn't enough. With the memory of my mother's sad widowed years stuck in my head, I threw myself into trying to make connections.

I joined the recreation center nearby and took a yoga class. I joined Meetup.com and found a history walking-tour group, a movie group and a critical thinking group. With some trepidation, I dined and danced with total strangers and met people who were as anxious as I. The experiences varied. I enjoyed the movie meetups but was repelled by the archery class run by post-apocalyptic survivalists. Yet it was all about learning to socialize as a single again.

Although I didn't have any dates and didn't want any, the activities gave me something to look forward to and people of my own age with whom I could speak.

Socializing vs. Solitude

A lot of how-to articles encourage, in fact stress, socializing as being vital for some people. That would be me. But there are people who love endless hours of solitude to read, write, paint or tinker with their train sets, happily spending days at a time without seeing anyone else.

The Mather Institute, which researches and reports on aging, divides seniors into solitude seekers and social seekers, two quite different groups.

"Positive motivations for solitude," a Mather report states, *"are unlikely to pose risks for older adults and are associated with levels of wellbeing comparable to people who prefer greater levels of social interaction."*

So if you're a person who loves being alone and have positive motivations for doing so, that's wonderful. Positive motivations would mean perhaps having creative activities, like writing poetry or painting, traveling or dining alone.

On the other hand, if the motivations are negative, because of social anxiety, depression or other factors, it would be unhealthy and professional help might be necessary.

The Optimism Factor

In my experience, women seem to fare better than men when they find themselves single later in life. But optimism can be a factor that's equally important as gender. A study by the Women's Health Initiative in 2022 found that women of all races with higher levels of optimism had a longer lifespan. Negativity leads to poorer health and a shorter lifespan, the research shows. That makes sense. Who wants to have a long life if it's going to be negative, anyway?

Apart from cutting into our longevity, negativity is a dead giveaway for unhappiness. If you find yourself having negative or cynical thoughts for an extended period after becoming single, something is wrong and it's time to examine the causes.

Some people associate becoming single late in life, especially after a divorce or breakup, as an embarrassment. They've failed in their search for love. They feel guilty about their status, avoiding old friends and sinking into habits that might be harmful.

Framing a Positive Perspective

Even if the gloom is manageable, as it was in my case, it takes a mental effort to start getting active again and you'll need motivation. We're talking about a mental paradigm shift that allows you to frame your situation differently. Viewing it from another perspective can be a huge game changer.

First, you have to talk yourself into seeing your newfound status in a positive, optimistic light. I used to tell myself, so you're single again. It's not the end of the world. Here's an opportunity to be anything you want, to do anything you want. Just get on with it. Even if I couldn't throw my grief to the side, had to carry it like a leaky bucket that would get lighter with time, I had to believe there was a brighter future ahead.

Time for Action

You may have nothing to grieve at this point but you've decided you want companionship. Maybe you've been dating online for a while, had disappointing results and want to learn something new that might help you. Maybe someone has given you the book to encourage you to seek a partner. No matter the reason for reading these words, I applaud you for even thinking of doing things differently. Before you look outward for a special friend, however, you'll have to look within and ask the question, Am I really prepared for a new chapter in my life?

When you've been alone for a long time, you can start to become sloppy and unhealthy in your habits. Sometimes you start indulging in bad habits that guarantee running into trouble with or without a partner. Living in sweat suits, staying up past bedtime and eating junk food won't make you a desirable mate. It's so important, whether you plan to date or not, to check yourself when you realize that's happened and practice self-care.

You can turn your life into an adventure at any age. But you have to prepare for it. This is the perfect opportunity to review your current lifestyle and ask yourself, how can I better nurture myself to prepare for the adventures ahead? The questions on the following page will help you to do the self-analysis you need to get the journey started.

Chapter One Checklist

Think about the changes you might need to make your quality of life even better.

(If relevant) Have I grieved adequately? Y/N If no, what else can I do?

....

....

Do I have feelings from past relationships that would affect my ability to date?

....

....

Do I view my single status positively or negatively?

....

....

Am I in the best physical and mental shape to date right now? Y/N   Why or why not?

....

....

Do I need to change my eating habits? Y/N   If yes, how?

....

....

Do I need to sleep more or less? No/More/Less   If more or less, what should I do?

....

....

Do I get enough exercise? Y/N   If no, how can I improve on that?

....

....

Do I need to get out of the house more? Y/N

....

....

Do I need to socialize more? Y/N   If yes, how?

....

....

What else can I do to get myself in the best possible shape?

....

....

Chapter Two
Becoming Resilient

There are no guarantees that after reading this book you'll find the partner you envision. You might have dates that don't go the way you want and you have to be able to bounce back, no matter the disappointment. In fact, if you're going to enjoy the time you have left on earth with or without a partner, you have to be resilient. So, before we get into dating, let's look at what it takes to live well at our age.

First let me say I love the word *resilience*. It sounds strong but flexible, sexy but practical. It just sounds like bamboo, able to bend and adapt while staying firmly grounded.

The word has been popping up a lot recently with multiple studies proving that people who are resilient lead happier, longer lives. If you're making choices about your love life, being happy, healthy and adaptable will matter. You don't want to settle into a wonderful partnership only to find it crumbling because of bad habits or poor health. Believe me, I know. Not looking after yourself, not having the courage to do the hard stuff, can destroy you.

I had a high school classmate who was known in school for her dry, plain-talking wit. When I met up with her at a re-union when we were both about 35, I was shocked. Her hair

11

was in a severe bun, she had lines on her face and she looked haggard. What had happened to my friend? She was married to an alcoholic, she said. And, no, she wasn't leaving him even though his drinking was ruining her life as well as his. She seemed to be more concerned with taking care of him — and forgetting to take care of herself.

I have the airlines to thank for reminding me on every trip that you have to put on your own oxygen mask first before you can help another passenger.

Gumption

The interaction with my classmate has served as my personal example of where I never want to be and I've often wondered why my response was so different from hers. Maybe because my mother said you need *pluck* to face your problems and my father talked about *gumption*. Since both my parents had challenging younger lives but managed to stay married to the end, they knew what it took.

After my fiancé died, a friend comforted me by saying I would get through my grief because I was resilient, so resilient that I should write a book about it. She summarized my previous twelve months: I'd had Covid, witnessed my car go up in flames, sold my home, left an academic job, moved to a strange town, moved in with my fiancé — and discovered him dead six months later. And now, she added, you're moving again, buying a home and getting on with your life.

Resilient? Not until then did I realize that the word applied to me.

The Arizona Center on Healthy and Resilient Aging's research has shown that there's a strong connection between a higher rate of happiness in older adults compared to the general population, and they conclude that it's related to resilience. After job losses, deaths, moving homes, losing homes, most elders end up more contented with their lives. Being resilient leads to their mental, emotional and physical wellbeing, helping them to survive crises. They were able to bend — and bounce back.

I understand some people's frustration being told by a bunch of experts to be resilient when you don't know how to do it. Some even say, I wasn't born resilient, that's just not me. But no one is born resilient. It's a skill we learn at any age, a skill we absolutely should learn, because it gets us through the worst that life can throw at us.

Learning Resilience

There's an informative book by gerontologist Karl Pillemer of Cornell University called *Thirty Lessons for Living*. Dr. Pillemer interviewed over a thousand 90 and 100-year-olds to find out why they had survived so well and lived so long despite going through wars, the Holocaust, multi-country migration, the loss of everything they possessed and the deaths of loved ones.

Dr. Pillemer was able to narrow these elders' techniques for surviving crises down to four:

- **They took the long view**. They reminded themselves that this too shall pass, life will go on. And they kept repeating it until they believed it.
- **They prepared instead of worried.** They took action where they could. Becoming part of the solution left them feeling empowered and less stressed.
- **They were kind to others.** Kindness gave them a positive boost and sent out a message of hope, making everyone feel better.
- **They enjoyed small daily pleasures**. Staying in the moment, enjoying nature, hobbies or other people lifted them, even temporarily, out of whatever gloom they were experiencing.

To double down on that last point, Viktor Frankl, a psychiatrist who survived the concentration camps of World War II, wrote in *Man's Search for Meaning* that when he picked a wild flower as they were marched to the fields, it gave him the boost he needed to get through another horrific day.

According to Dr. Pillemer, it's possible for anyone to learn how to be resilient. Based on his research of these elders, he says we should:

- Maintain an optimistic attitude and always look for the "silver lining."
- Engage in new activities.
- Cultivate new friendships or join a social group.
- Accept that some things are out of our control, and take action on the things we can affect.
- Practice stress-management techniques.
- Develop a spiritual practice like prayer, meditation, yoga or mindful journaling.
- Maintain perspective; don't let our thoughts run away with us.
- Practice self-care through proper nutrition, regular exercise and good sleep habits.
- Volunteer our time to help others.
- Ask for help when we need it.
- And look for the lessons in every situation.

That's a long list! But we'll break it down to something more digestible at the end of the chapter. What we want to make sure of is that we're on the right path with practices that become second nature, leading to a satisfying, engaged and, yes, resilient life.

Resilient Dating

Apart from being needed when you find yourself alone, resilience will carry you through the inevitable stressors of aging, with or without a relationship. And being resilient, reminding yourself of the techniques to get there, will jump you over your problems and bring you back to normalcy quicker.

That's especially true when you want to find a partner. I've heard seniors say they want a relationship but can't take the stress. Every relationship brings stress. But it's being able to move through that stress that will make a relationship stronger. Running away from your wish to be involved romantically or dropping a partner at the first sign of conflict will not get you where you want.

Solving the inevitable problems makes a partnership stronger. Having a win-win approach to conflicts, staying with the issue and not bringing up the past, finding common ground, are all ways to remove or reduce the conflict and form a better

16

bond. And even if you choose not to date, you'll still need to be resilient to get through the times you'll be facing alone.

Dating takes courage. As you go through the frog-kissing process, there might be times when you're anxious, or when someone rejects you, when you have to hurt someone's feelings, or when you discover you've been scammed. As with everything worth having in life, there are going to be hurdles to vault. Let's be resilient enough to get up and over the hurdles!

Chapter Two Checklist

Here's a list of questions for you based on Dr. Pillimer's suggestions for being resilient.

What can I have a better attitude about?

....

....

What action could I have taken in the past or take now to change a negative situation?

....

....

What spiritual practice feels comfortable to me? When/where can I start practicing it?

....

....

Which thoughts have I allowed to run away with me? How could I shift perspective?

....

....

What act of kindness can I do within the next 24 hours?

....

....

What new stress management techniques can I adopt?

....

....

What lesson did I learn from a recent negative situation?

....

....

Do I ask for help when I need it? Why or why not?

....

....

(If necessary) Where else should I seek help?

....

....

....

....

....

....

Chapter Three
Going for the End Goal

When we find ourselves single late in life, most of us make a decision about partnership, consciously or not. But the yellow brick road to happiness can be confusing. Our parents might not have dressed in black like widows in the Mediterranean, but in generations past they often turned into home-bound hermits after they became divorced or widowed. Luckily, today's elders have a smorgasbord of mating possibilities for their later years.

The Many Relationship Options

I personally know seniors who have chosen to:

- Flirt around on dating websites, but never actually date.
- Socialize with a circle of friends but rule out dating.
- Enjoy platonic dates and leave it at that.
- Have brief sexual affairs but choose to stay single and alone.
- Enjoy a long-term, monogamous relationship where both partners live separately.
- Live with a partner with no intention of marrying.

- Go the traditional route of dating and marrying.
- Maintain a long-distance relationship.
- Marry but live in separate houses.

These choices may be temporary, like the grandparent who focuses on caring for a young grandchild, then looks for a mate when the child starts school. Some stick quite happily with one choice.

What you don't want is to be unhappily stuck in a rut. I knew a woman who longed for a partner but was too scared to seek one, fearful he might turn out to be a rapist, murderer or womanizer. Still remembering the betrayal of her ex-husband, she wouldn't allow herself to become vulnerable again and chose to remain single for lonely decades after her divorce.

Another retired acquaintance became a host extraordinaire after his breakup. Always planning the next party or bike ride or trivia contest, he rarely had time for himself and, even though he wanted to have a partner, used his busyness to avoid men who could hurt him again. For both of these folks, fear prevented them from evolving.

The Choice to Date

Not everyone needs a relationship, true. I'd never tell a seeker of solitude, someone who thoroughly enjoys their own company, that they should socialize or date. If they're happy, there's no reason to change. But since I assume you're considering having a partner, let's take a closer look at this process we call dating.

As you see from the list above, dating can take many forms, from sexual to platonic, from short- to long-term. Self-examination is essential when choosing how to date. Clearly identifying what feels right for you will put you ahead of the game and save time.

Don't put off asking the hard questions. Digging deep will result in a more focused approach to dating. This is when you ask yourself if there's time in your life to date, because maybe an occasional date would work if you're a busy person.

Do you want a platonic relationship? Are you happy with your lifestyle and don't want to give it up? Would you prefer a long-term relationship without commitment? Do you want to get married? It's best to play it straight with yourself and your prospective partner from the beginning. You don't want to raise expectations only to have them crushed later.

The Positives of Dating

I'm going to avoid the negative arguments about dating: the loss of independence, the need for compromise. The list can be endless and somewhat discouraging. Since you've started reading this book, I want to look at the positives, in case you still have doubts about dating. From my own experience I've found that, first, dating provides companionship, another human being with whom to share activities, thoughts and feelings. If you don't like being alone all the time, that's a nice change. Second, it feels good to hug and kiss, even without sex; humans need touch. Third, compliments and positive feedback from your partner reinforce good feelings about yourself and raise self-esteem. Fourth, you can expand your circle of friends and get exposure to new people, cultures and perspectives.

There are some really good scientific reasons for seniors to date. Remember that good feeling when you're flirting? That's your seratonin flooding the brain, the hormone which makes you feel happy. And now they've discovered that committed, longer relationships are even healthier for us than just a passing flirtation.

Harry Reis, PhD, co-editor of *The Encyclopedia of Human Relationships,* says that, although short-term relationships can be stressful, long-term relationships have a wide variety of health benefits. A good partnership impacts our heart health, for instance. A publication of the American Psychological Association ran an article about research conducted at the University of Rochester that showed that "happily wedded people who undergo coronary bypass surgery are more than three times as likely to be alive 15 years later as their unmarried counterparts."

Other studies have shown that having a strong partnership lowers blood pressure, results in fewer colds and allows us to manage our stress better. So if you want the benefits of a loving relationship, you'll have to turn off Amazon Prime, get off the couch and date.

Caution Ahead

Not all dates end in warm, fuzzy feelings. First, I would warn against high expectations. Infatuation before knowing someone well can lead to heart break. Second, we can ignore the red flags and get involved with unsavory characters. Third, we can open ourselves to being manipulated or scammed. Fourth, we can be hurt or rejected.

Although we don't want to be frozen in fear, we need to be familiar with the tell-tale signs of a bad partnership. Our happiness, sometimes our money or our life, might depend on it. We have to guard our hearts!

When you start dating, please heed the following signs.

- **Bad habits.** If your date smokes and you do not, for example, you need to ask yourself if you want to put up with it.
- **Physical abuse**. A date might touch you in a way that feels unpleasant. If ignored, this can accelerate into pushing, slapping or worse.
- **Emotional or verbal abuse.** This might include posting social media comments, photographs or videos of you, as well as making intimidating or degrading comments.
- **Drug or alcohol abuse.** A date can become unpleasant or aggressive or encourage you to join in their excesses.
- **Economic exploitation**. Whether it is online dating scammers or a con man or woman, they're out there and vulnerable seniors are regularly targeted.
- **Unwanted sexual contact.** One person might feel pressured to go along with their partner's demands although they don't want to.

Dating isn't always peaches and cream. There are ogres out there of both genders, of all ages and races. If you're going to have a good dating experience, your eyes need to be wide open from the start. Even if you think you're in love, listen to the feedback from those you trust. When a date leaves you stressed, disappointed or upset, it's best to stop seeing that person. Eventually it will get easier to snap back to your best self, because you'll become more resilient each time.

It's okay to delay dating to ask questions and make wise choices, and it's okay to pull the plug on dating if you need a time out. What's not okay is to want a partner but not move forward to date because you're too scared.

If you choose to date, focus on making it a fun, healthy and productive experience. You might even make some good friends along the way. Remember, nothing ventured, nothing gained.

Chapter Three Checklist

What are *your* relationship end goals? Time for some soul searching.

Am I happiest when I'm alone for long periods? Y/N If no, when are you happiest?

....

....

Do I feel lonely now? Y/N If yes, how can you change that?

....

....

....

Do I genuinely want to find a partner? Y/N Why/why not?

....

....

....

Have I avoided finding a partner because I'm afraid? Y/N
If yes, what are you afraid of?

....

....

....

Do I want a short- or long-term relationship? ST/LT   Why?

....

....

....

....

Do I prefer a monogamous relationship or multiple concurrent relationships?   Mono/Multi   Why?

....

....

....

....

How do I feel about getting married?

....

....

....

....

....

....

Chapter Four
Thriving with Senior Sex

A few years ago I was chatting with my best man-friend, pretending not to notice the 40 pounds that chemo had taken away, when he leaned towards me, lowering his voice. I'm still looking for real love, passionate love, he said, to experience it just once. It wasn't the first time he'd said that, but this time I wanted to yell at my 78-year-old buddy, Are you crazy? You're dying! Six months later, lying in a hospital bed, the only word he could utter to me was "Home." Passion forgotten, all he wanted were his family and native country, where he died shortly after.

The idea of passion, sex by another name, often dominates discussions about modern partnership. Sometimes it seems like sexual attraction is more important than companionship or common sense. And for some people like my friend, the urge may never decline.

Health Benefits

As we're hearing more and more, there are physical advantages to sex. The Society of Obstetricians and Gynecologists of Canada reports that sex for seniors:

- Minimizes the risk of incontinence;
- Helps you sleep by easing the body and lulling the mind and spirit;
- Lowers the risk of prostate cancer;
- Decreases blood pressure by opening and relaxing the blood vessels;
- Releases human growth hormones which, along with the discharge of some estrogen and testosterone, are key factors in keeping your skin elastic, reducing wrinkles, firming muscles, shining the skin and making your hair softer; and
- Diminishes atrophy or shrinkage of the prostate and vagina and other muscles and ligaments.

No wonder the TV series *Grace and Frankie* is so popular with seniors since that's often the subject!

Taboo Talk

Yet when two Baby Boomers date, sex is often the unspoken elephant in the room. It's ironic that Boomers, the most sexually liberated generation, often find themselves tongue-tied speaking about the topic, even to their children. I'm no exception. My daughter accuses me of not educating her about sex, just handing her a book. She's right. I never learned how to talk about sex. When I asked my mother how it felt to have a man penetrate you — I was about fourteen — all she said was, It's the best thing since sliced bread. I never did make the connection between bread and sex.

I remember, somewhat nostalgically I confess, a time when the subject of older people having sex was taboo. When my grandfather remarried in his fifties, no one dreamed that the newlyweds would indulge. In fact, I never heard any discussion in my family about sex. Ever.

Nothing seems taboo anymore. Teenage videos of private parts are uploaded to social media, children become sexually active at younger ages and so-called family movies often include sexual innuendo. And it's not only kiddy sex. Now that Boomers have aged, having lived through the lusty 1970s and 80s, senior sex with its many issues, from erectile dysfunction to vaginal dryness, has become the topic of commercials, talk shows, documentaries and articles — to the point of being mundane. We're constantly being reminded that illness, disability, medications or surgery can affect sexual desire and intimacy.

Men are urged to take meds for erectile dysfunction because you've got to have sex to be happy, according to the ads. Being okay with our declining libido is unacceptable, apparently, and we're supposed to fight nature. So loaded is the pressure for seniors to have sex that some pretend they're still having sex when they're not, and some pretend they don't want it when they do.

There's bad news and good news when it comes to the facts. Research from the National Poll on Healthy Aging showed that 40 percent of people ages 65 to 80 were sexually active. That's just an average, and sexual activity declines with age. Nearly three-quarters of people 65 to 80 have a partner, married or not, and only half of those are sexually active. The good news is that while half of older marriages are asexual, two-thirds of all seniors say they're interested in having sex, according to the poll. They might not be having it, but they're interested!

Unfortunately, sex can be an impediment to some seniors who would like to have a partner. They don't want to be embarrassed by having to admit they no longer have sexual urges or they've had an illness or surgery that makes it difficult or impossible. Many never seek medical advice on the subject, assuming they should no longer have sex or can't have sex. It's important to get advice from a professional if you feel a desire for a partner but are conflicted, because there are now all kinds of modern techniques, including vibrators, injections and medication, to improve your sex life.

Is it just Lust?

Of course, sex should be differentiated from lust. As far as online dating goes, some people select a person to contact based purely on looks. They're attracted to someone pretty, sexy and often younger. (I hear a chorus of women shout, Yes!) And you don't have to have a high libido to get excited by someone's looks. I've asked men about this and they say, I'm physically attracted first, then I look at their personality.

I won't generalize and call all men lustful, but there are scientific theories about why men are initially attracted to looks (survival of the race, etc.). My only comment is that if a man doesn't intend to start a family, choosing a partner based on looks alone will limit his options.

In all fairness to men, we need to talk about women. According to researchers who connect our partner selection process to ancient needs, women look primarily for men who have status in the tribe, men who can protect and support a family. Many older women today seek out men who are financially stable and look like leaders.

Yet women seek attractive men, too, which is why online scammers use profile photographs of handsome men to draw women in. Senior women will sometimes raise an eyebrow at a guy after he passes or make jokes about a footballer's rear end. What about the woman with a passionate relationship with a nicely toned stud?

Older women marrying younger men is no longer eyebrow-raising, especially after celebrities like Tina Turner and Mary Tyler Moore proved that it can work. As I said, there are all kinds of options available. For both genders.

Libido

If you don't have strong sexual or physical urges, don't despair. Don't assume that you're done with sex. The National Institutes of Health reported in a study of seniors back in 2007 that half of their respondents had at least two bothersome sexual problems, mostly erectile dysfunction in men and apathy and dryness in women. But both can be overcome now.

Ten years later, *The Lancet*, a scientific journal that studies health in seniors, reported that more than half of sexually active people between 75 and 85 years old had sex two to three times per month, and 25 percent once a week or more.

It's never too late, and you never know what might turn you on. I have a friend who thought he'd never have another erection, until he met a woman who excited him and they ended up having a whale of a time!

The Talk

Now let's look at the elephant in the room: the often unspoken question between seniors getting to know each other: What about sex? The tension can be caused for several reasons, perhaps because you're worried the other person might not want sex and you do. Or because you have health issues or think you can't have sex.

Dating websites try to handle this dilemma by having you check off the type of relationship you're looking for: romance or friendship, short-term or long-term, serious or casual. They seldom mention sex. You have to read between the lines when you look at other people's profiles to guess if romance includes celibacy, or if friendship means a passing fling.

Even before you go online or on that first date, you should be clear with yourself about your intentions. Are you seeking a platonic companion or a sexual partner? If you move forward with the relationship, the issue will come up sooner or later. But don't rush it. Give the relationship a chance to evolve because timing is key.

Don't assume you're turning the other person on with sex talk; you're just setting yourself up to be dumped. There are some hilarious stories about bad timing for sex talk. Here are some examples of when NOT to talk about your prowess or expectations:

- To an attractive cashier at the supermarket
- To an acquaintance between pickle ball games
- On a cruise to another dinner guest
- To your server in a restaurant
- On your dating website profile
- In the first phone call to a potential date
- On your first in-person date

Those early dates are about two strangers getting to know each other's personalities, core values, likes and dislikes. Strangers don't want to hear about your medical issues, and they may feel uncomfortable talking about sex too soon. Trying to ferret out the other person's medical history or sharing your history of STDs are a definite no-no, and asking if he/she uses Viagra or a vibrator not only ensures rejection but a post-date snicker with friends. Plus, there are huge privacy issues when it comes to this information.

Sexually Transmitted Diseases

According to the Centers for Disease Control, the rate of sexually transmitted infections has shot up over the last few years. They reported that between 2014 and 2018 the number of cases of gonorrhea rose 164 percent among Americans age 55 and older, while cases of syphilis rose 120 percent and chlamydia rose 86 percent. And one of the communities with the fastest growing rate of STDs in the country is an over-55 community in Florida. That's shocking news to many.

Of course, if you have a sexually transmitted disease, I would urge you not to date until you've cleared up or controlled the situation. And you should tell your partner about your status before you move into a sexual relationship. In many states it's mandatory that you disclose that you have HIV or AIDS before having sex.

Health issues should also be revealed if they impact your sexual life. If you conceal the important stuff, it will cause trouble down the line when the truth comes out.

Not too soon and not too late, that's the rule on talking about sex when you start dating. Be patient and the time to have that discussion will arise naturally. So don't rush it — but don't avoid it if you plan on having sex eventually.

Chapter Four Checklist

Please answer the following questions honestly. You're the only person who'll read it.

Are you sexually active? Y/N If no, would you like to be?

....

....

Do you have health issues that prohibit sex? Y/N What are they?

....

....

Have you spoken to a professional about your sex life? Y/N If so, what have they said?

....

....

Do you date or would you consider dating? Y/N If no, you can discontinue the checklist.

....

....

Would you rule out a celibate partnership? Y/N   Explain why.

....

....

When will you discuss the subject of sex with a prospective partner, and how?

....

....

Would you use a sex aid (Viagra, vibrator, etc.) during sex? How do you feel about using them?

....

....

What changes would you make to improve your sex life?

....

....

....

....

....

Chapter Five
Considering Online Dating

We've all heard stories about people who rekindle high school romances decades later, or of a couple who find love in a nursing home and marry at the age of 95.

But in practical terms if you don't have a long-lost love or you're not ready for a nursing home, what do you do?

A friend recently asked me what was the best way to meet a man. I said, Try a dating website. After trying out a website someone else recommended, she scoffed at the idea. I sent her a link to an app for people who had a lot in common with her and she loved it.

While for young people digital anything comes naturally, seniors aren't always friends of technology. If, according to The Senior List website, 26 percent of seniors over 65 are planning to date, are they using dating websites?

Like my friend, many find it aggravating to have to resort to a virtual world to find a partner. But it works. If it didn't, the industry wouldn't be booming.

Seniors in the Online Dating World

Online dating exploded after 2016, along with the number of dating apps and the money they're bringing in. Statista, a website that stores dating stats, says that in 2022 there were 57 million users in the US.

Approximately 46 percent of all internet users in the country have used dating apps, and it's pretty even by race, with 29 percent White, 31 percent Black and 28 percent Latino usage. Young folks, right? Mostly, but look again.

According to a Pew Research Center report in 2023, 13 percent of people over 65 use dating apps. If 40 percent of seniors are single, that means about 33 percent of people over 65 are dating online, or at least looking. The rest are wondering if they should and if it's safe.

That feeds into Pew's findings that 62 percent of Americans ages 65 and older think online dating is unsafe, compared with 53 percent of those 50 to 64, and 42 percent of adults younger than 50. Those who have never used a dating site are particularly likely to think it's unsafe: 57 percent compared with 32 percent of those who *have* used an online dating site.

What do these numbers prove? That the anxiety about online dating declines when we use it.

Embracing Online Dating

If fear has kept you from online dating, maybe you'd see things differently if you tried it. Granted it takes time to get accustomed to it, deciding what messages to answer and which to ignore, but if you're serious about finding a mate you should reconsider.

There's no guarantee you'll meet someone to fit your needs, but you might.

The main advantage to going online is the size of the dating pool. There are a lot of fish in that pond who want to be caught, so take advantage of that. You'll never be able to meet thousands of seniors going about your normal day. In fact, if you have a routinized life, you might just be meeting the same unsuitable or unavailable people over and over again. Throw your fishing hook into the bigger pond and take a chance.

You might be meeting people playing bridge at the recreation center, but why not try multiple ways to find your right person? There's no law saying you can't join a ballroom dance class at the same time that you're using a dating website. Think about expanding your options.

The good news is that, according to Forbes magazine in a 2021 article, about two-thirds, or 66 percent, of seniors using dating apps or websites had a relationship with someone they met through the platform. A pretty great result, I'd say.

Choosing the Right Website

You might now be curious about online dating, but you'll need to do some research, starting with verbal recommendations. If you have friends who have gone online to date, ask them about their experiences. Get familiar with the different websites and read reviews about them. Some are free, others are not. But remember, you'll get what you pay for.

From my two decades of experience with dating online, I've found out the hard way that it's best to subscribe to a site, because anybody, and I mean anybody, can join a free dating site. I've seen homeless folks in the public library on free dating websites. If people have to pay to join, it rules out the freeloaders, some of them, anyway.

The website rating service www.mindbodygreen.com ranks the popular sites for seniors and the reasons for their selection as:

- eHarmony (best overall)
- Silver Singles (best for seniors on a budget)
- Our Time (best designed for seniors)
- Hinge (for people of color over 50)
- Match (for serious relationships)
- Tinder (casual dating)
- OkCupid (shared interests)

At last count there were over 8,000 websites that served senior daters, including specialized ones for academics, retired professionals, Muslims, gays, Hindus, Christians, African Americans, Latinos, LGBTQ folks, dog lovers, cat lovers, farmers, you name it.

Take a look online before deciding and read the reviews, good and bad, before settling on one.

Experiment and Stay Cautious

If you're still a bit wary of online dating, I'd suggest you experiment for a short while. You can often sign up for a 30-day trial free of charge. Thirty days is going to give you an idea about how the system works, but bear in mind that it will take some time, perhaps months, to find a suitable date that you actually meet in person. And if you decide not to subscribe to the site, remember to cancel it completely because they will go ahead and charge your credit card for the next month. They're in this for money not love, trust me.

There are multiple reasons why you may decide not to proceed with online dating. You might be discouraged by all the doom and gloom stories about widows who have lost their fortunes to scammers and people who have been murdered by their date. But remember, these cases are a drop in the bucket compared to the folks who have had more positive experiences.

Over the decades that I've used online sites, I've had two unpleasant experiences. One was a man who was furious because he expected me to pay for my own dinner but said nothing throughout, and another with a man who was rude and controlling to the waiter and to me. Plus his photographs were taken when he was much younger.

Yes, there are con artists on dating apps, but I'll show you how to avoid them if you keep reading. There are plenty of successful and happy matches to balance out all those negatives, don't worry.

The Positives Win

What are the other stories to counter the scary stuff you've heard? A website called www.datingadvice.com cites research studies showing that:

- People who meet online get married quicker
- Over 17 percent of marriages start with online dating
- Marriages that start with online contact are less likely to end in the first year than other marriages
- Married couples who initially met online report greater satisfaction than other couples

Even if these facts are somewhat biased and include daters of all ages, they're worth noting. I've also heard of research that says that marriages that start with online dating don't last as long as other marriages and other research saying they're about the same. Take your pick.

Most importantly, you need to decide if you're willing to take the plunge, and don't let me or anyone else pressure you into doing so. Do your homework until you feel comfortable with your final decision.

Chapter Five Checklist

To ensure you're making the right choice, answer the following questions.

Do I feel conflicted about dating online? Y/N   Why or why not?

....

....

Is there another route to meeting a partner that I prefer? Y/N If yes, what route?

....

....

If I want to go online, am I prepared to do the research beforehand? Y/N   How?

....

....

What have I heard about online dating that makes me uncomfortable?

....

....

....

Do I prefer to experiment with online dating for a short period? Y/N   Why?

....

....

Do I feel pressured to date online? Y/N   Who or what makes me feel that way?

....

....

Am I ready to learn more about dating online? Y/N   Why?

....

....

....

....

Chapter Six
Finessing Your Profile

The hardest part of dating virtually is deciding to do it. After that, the website you've chosen will make it easy to get online. But not so fast.

Remember throughout the uploading process that:

- Scammers will see your profile as soon as it goes public.
- Honesty is the best policy because your readers and possible future dates will judge you on what you've written.
- DON'T overshare information.
- DO NOT send the message that you're lonely or wealthy.
- DO NOT reveal intimate, personal information.

After you've absorbed that, you can enter the website you've selected. You'll be asked to answer questions about yourself and about what you're looking for in a relationship. They're gradually luring you into a subscription, of course.

Be aware that most of what you enter will appear eventually on your profile page. It's important that you submit accurate information because trying to change what you originally wrote can be a hassle later.

Your Written Information

Either before or after you've uploaded your photographs, you'll be asked to write about who you are and what you're looking for in a partner. Here are some more do's and don'ts for that written part of your profile.

- **DO fill out the written portions of your profile.** Don't leave them blank. It's important to let people into your world, clarify who you're looking for and rule out partners you don't want.

- **DO write the truth**. Back pedaling later to make corrections will make your date feel you can't be trusted.

- **DO keep your writing brief.** But not too brief.

- **DO use humor if you know how to do it.** A witty narrative will make readers chuckle and want to get to know you.

- **DO avoid sensitive topics** that might be offensive to others, like politics, race, religion, etc.

- **DON'T give detailed information about yourself or where you live.**

- **DON'T post immediately if you don't write well.** Ask someone knowledgeable to edit it first.

- **DON'T reveal your financial information.** You'll only encourage freeloaders and scammers.

- **DON'T talk about your medical issues.** Everyone has them at our age.

51

- **DON'T sound as if you're desperate for a relationship.** Keep it light and cheerful.

Uploading Your Photographs

Next you will be asked to upload photographs onto your profile page. Here are some do's and don'ts about posting pictures.

- **DO use several photographs.** Your viewers want to see you in multiple settings and from different perspectives.
- **DO use clear, well-taken photos.**
- **DO show yourself engaged in hobbies you enjoy**, like being in nature, fishing or traveling. If you do something creative, like painting, show some of your work.
- **DO include a photo of your pet if you have one.** Some people are allergic or don't want to be around animals.
- **DO use photographs taken within the last year.** You don't want your date to be disappointed because your photos are ten years old.
- **DON'T use old photographs!** This is so important I've put it in both do's and don'ts.
- **DON'T post hurried photos.** I'm talking about selfies of yourself reflected in a mirror. That's just lazy, as is taking a photograph with your laptop.
- **DON'T use blurry, off-center photos.** You'll only get emails from a scammer.

- **DON'T show yourself nude or in a suggestive pose**. It's tasteless and you might be kicked off the website.
- **DON'T have shots of yourself with lots of friends.** Your prospective date only wants to see you — and maybe your children or grandchildren.

After you've done the work of writing your profile and uploading photos, you may be asked to subscribe to join the website. You then have to decide on the time period you will be signing on to. I recommend a three-month subscription so you can try it out. Who knows? You might want to switch to another website after that period.

Once you've paid up, there might be a short waiting period while the website reviews it. They're trying to rule out pornography and scamming as best they can. In the meanwhile, you'll be able to search for prospective dates. This is the fun part, when you get to look at other people's profiles, thinking, Hmmm, she/he looks interesting.

I need to add, please don't write anyone or answer incoming emails until you've read the next chapter on scammers. Their tactics are clever and they change year after year. You need to read as much as you can about the huge scamming industry, because these guys (and some are female) are good.

After you know how to avoid scammers, you'll be ready to do some partner shopping.

Chapter Six Checklist

Let's check if you're ready for your virtual debut. Answer these questions before you click the submit button.

Have I uploaded photographs taken within the last year? Y/N How many?

....

....

Do my photographs show me from different angles? Y/N

....

....

Are the photographs clear and attractive? Y/N

....

....

In my writing, have I been brief but not too brief? Y/N

....

....

Have I omitted my financial, sexual, legal and other personal information? Y/N

....

....

Does my profile make me sound lonely and in need of a relationship? Y/N

....

....

Do I sound confident and optimistic throughout? Y/N

....

....

....

....

....

Chapter Seven
Dissing the Scammers

efore you launch into the online dating world, you have to learn to protect yourself from fraud. The Federal Trade Commission estimates that between 2017 and 2021 scammers netted more than $1.3 billion just in online dating sites. You don't want your assets added to that number. I almost did and it served as a huge lesson for me.

Pew Research Center, my favorite resource, found that in 2022 about half of all seniors who dated online thought they had encountered someone who had tried to scam them.

Senior singles make perfect targets for scammers, particularly if you're a widow or appear lonely, both of which make you vulnerable, and the vultures will come down as soon as your profile is made public. To avoid being defrauded, you've got to recognize profiles and emails that are not authentic and reject the advances of scammers immediately.

Romance Scamming

Romance scamming is the term used to describe the industry that attacks online daters. There are banks of scammers in different countries sitting at computer screens creating fake profiles and writing fake emails to online daters.

Several websites, including government agencies, can give you advice about how to recognize a romance scam. The one I use most is the FBI's website. They even have a page to report an online scam and I've used it myself once. When I told the scammer I was reporting him to the FBI, he slammed the phone down.

I was new to online dating when that happened. I'd received an email from a man whose profile had a single photograph. Since he looked attractive, I got intrigued and we started communicating. He was supposed to be an engineer who was born in Germany and, although he lived in the US, he was currently working in a distant country. We corresponded for a while and then agreed to talk on the phone. When the man called, I surprised him by speaking in German. Only then, when my caller was unable to reply in German, did I realize I was being scammed. The attractive photograph had been phished, or copied, off the internet.

Now I report the scammer to the dating website immediately so they can investigate. They can look at the emails and kick the scammer off the site.

FBI Website on Romance Scamming

The FBI has a great website that senior singles looking to date online should use. I urge you to look at it before answering or approaching anyone on a dating app. I've taken the following information directly from their site:

- Romance scams occur when a criminal adopts a fake online identity to gain a victim's affection and trust. The scammer then uses the illusion of a romantic or close relationship to manipulate and/or steal from the victim.

- The criminals who carry out romance scams are experts at what they do and will seem genuine, caring, and believable. Con artists are present on most dating/social media sites.

- The scammer's intention is to establish a relationship as quickly as possible, endear himself to the victim, and gain trust. Scammers may propose marriage and make plans to meet in person, but that will never happen. Eventually, they will ask for money.

- Scam artists often say they are in the building and construction industry and are engaged in projects outside the U.S. That makes it easier to avoid meeting in person – and more plausible when they ask for money for a medical emergency or unexpected legal fee.

- If someone you meet online needs your bank account information to deposit money, they are most likely using your account to carry out other theft and fraud schemes.

FBI Tips for Avoiding Scams

- Be careful what you post and make public online. Scammers can use details shared on social media and dating sites to better understand and target you.
- Research the person's photo and profile using online searches to see if the image, name, or details have been used elsewhere.
- Go slowly and ask lots of questions.
- Beware if the individual seems too perfect or quickly asks you to leave a dating service or social media site to communicate directly.
- Beware if the individual attempts to isolate you from friends and family or requests inappropriate photos or financial information that could later be used to extort you.
- Beware if the individual promises to meet in person but then always comes up with an excuse why he or she can't. If you haven't met the person after a few months, for whatever reason, you have good reason to be suspicious.
- Never send money to anyone you have only communicated with online or by phone.

Gillian's Scamming Tips

I have cues of my own that raise a red flag for me, telling me when someone is probably a scammer. At the risk of being repetitive, I'm going to include them.

There is usually only one photograph with the profile. If there are multiple photos, the person might be blurry or distant so you can't tell if it's the same person.

The English is poor with lots of punctuation errors. Your scammer says he/she is foreign born to cover for that problem.

The narrative is short and says little that's personal or unique. That's because the scammer uses the same wording in multiple emails to save time.

The profile uses romantic or generic cliches. 'I enjoy walking in the moonlight holding hands' is a popular one.

The scammer asks lots of questions. They want to get to know you as quickly as possible.

He or she will try to move you from the website to direct email or telephone quickly.

Remember, scammers usually live in poorer countries and you could be seen as wealthy and ripe for the rip-off. Keep your eyes open to protect yourself and cut off communication the second you suspect you're being conned. You'll quickly develop the skill of seeing through a scam and be able to move on to real relationships with real people.

Chapter Seven Checklist

Even if you feel uncomfortable judging people quickly, it's best to be suspicious right away rather than caught up in a scam. See if you can spot the profiles below that are possibly or definitely fake and check the answers on the following page.

1. Bob, great looking photo, builds bridges in Malaysia but comes originally from Italy.
2. Betty is from Norway, but her photo shows a woman with very curly hair.
3. Phillip jumps right in, calling you 'dear' in the first letter.
4. Sarah says she teaches English in a university but writes without periods or commas.
5. Rupert starts talking about a legal situation he finds himself in.
6. Cassandra asks lots of questions about your work, your family, your hobbies, etc.
7. Peter's profile says he believes that "love is a many splendored thing."
8. Diana accuses you of ignoring her letters.
9. Joseph wants you to write directly to his email instead of through the website.
10. Martha is a beauty of 35 (you're 75) and has a fabulous investment opportunity.

Answers to the Scam Spotter List

Were you able to spot your potential scammers? Your answers are below. Buckle up!

1. Bob doesn't have an Italian name. FAKE!
2. Betty doesn't look Norwegian. POSSIBLY FAKE!
3. Phillip is getting familiar too quickly. FAKE!
4. Sarah wouldn't be making grammar errors if she has an English degree. FAKE!
5. Rupert is working on your sympathy and is going to ask you for money. FAKE!
6. Cassandra needs to establish a bond so you'll feel like she's a trustworthy friend. FAKE!
7. Peter has copied and pasted the statement. POSSIBLY FAKE!
8. Diana is trying to make you feel guilty in order to manipulate you. FAKE!
9. Joseph knows that the website might catch on and delete his profile. FAKE!
10. Martha is heading for your wallet! FAKE!

Remember, it's better to be suspicious about everyone on a dating website until they've proven themselves to be authentic.

Chapter Eight
Diving into the Online Pool

You've sharpened your scammer chops and put up your profile... now you're ready for action. You wait a while, then you get a message from someone. Your heart beats faster — this could be the person, your Person.

This is where things get blurry. What do you say when you get a 'like' or a heart? If someone attracts your attention, should you write a long email telling them about yourself? Do you ignore a cheesy email that turns you off?

My advice is to move slowly when you first put up your profile. If you've never done this before, it can be a bit overwhelming. You might find yourself spending hours scrolling through the possible matches that the website sends you. Or you might write emails to folks you think are great matches but they never respond. Tamp your ego down and move on.

Toughening Up

Dating online means having a thick skin. There will probably be people who hurt your feelings and people whose feelings you hurt. It happens. And when it does, you can't take it personally and have to move on. Since your chance of finding the soul mate you've been looking for is about one percent (my personal guesstimate), it means that 99 percent of the people you communicate with will not be your soul mate. That's a lot of rejection.

Unfortunately, not everybody online has good manners. I once received several emails from a man who kept insisting that we were right for each other. Since I wasn't interested, I replied to his first email with a polite brush-off. But that didn't stop him. Although I never wrote him again, he kept up the pressure. He finally wrote accusing me of being snobbish and stuck up, you name it. Did he think that by insulting me he was increasing his chances of meeting me?

Not everybody is going to reply politely to your offer to meet for coffee. Not every online dater is going to think you're hot stuff. They'll be swiping past you for one reason or another, and you'll be doing the same with your matches. It's all part of the game, and if you don't have a tough skin it's time to grow one.

So if you're still planning to date online, I want you to say these words out loud: I WILL NOT TAKE ONLINE REJECTION PERSONALLY. You might need to repeat it. Only after you've accepted that mantra, will you be ready.

Then let the games begin.

You have Mail!

Your profile is up and an email from another member comes in. Here's a reality check: the first people to approach you on the website are often the scammers. Picture them lined up in their call centers or basements or wherever they hang out. They're online all the time, eagles waiting for the newbie dater to emerge from the nest. They're going to swoop in. That's how they earn their keep. But of course, you've read all about how to tell a scammer from a real dater and you reject those circling opportunists.

Waiting for the first real email to come in, you may wonder why you're not seeing any takers who want to approach you first. If that's the case, take a look at your profile and photographs and see if you're turning matches off. Ask friends to give you their honest feedback about what you've said about yourself and what you're looking for. Have you been harsh or bitter? Do the photographs make you look friendly, warm and approachable? Do they show you at your best?

You've gotten over that hump and now you receive your first heart or 'like.' Don't let it go to your head. There are men and women who send out a dozen hearts a day and think nothing of it.

When You're Approached

Usually when someone writes another person through a dating website, they'll say that they find your profile interesting and hope you'll reply. Do you respond? You don't have to. Take a look at the person's profile and decide. If they've taken the trouble to write an email and you're not attracted to them, you can politely and briefly reply that you appreciate it but aren't interested. Some people even say that they've decided to pursue another relationship and will therefore have to decline. No need for guilt either way.

On the other hand, maybe the person catches your attention and you want to continue communicating. Please take it slowly. My suggestion is get to know people first through their writing, then you can proceed to a phone call, followed by meeting in person. Each stage is there for a reason.

But first, notice how the person writes. Are they respectful of you? Do they have a sense of humor? These are all clues to their character and past experiences. When you write them back, don't give out details about where you live or work. Please! You don't want disturbed folks showing up at your front door. Writing those early emails should be only an indication of how a person thinks and feels, and that doesn't mean an autobiography.

Sometimes you might want to be the initiator of a match. Part of the fun of online dating, and I do mean fun, is scrolling through your matches using your search function, using a keyword like *travel*, for example, and finding someone intriguing who also likes to travel. In fact, I often pick my own matches and communicate with them first.

When You Write First

If you start the ball by writing someone you've seen online, remember to communicate in the same way that you would like someone to communicate with you. So in that first message you're going to:

- Be respectful at all times.
- Keep the first message brief and do not divulge anything personal.
- State only that you found their profile interesting and that you have things in common.
- Be specific by mentioning something in their profile that shows you've actually read it.
- Don't press the person you wrote if they don't answer back. Stop writing them!

Speaking in Person

When do you move on to a phone call? It depends. Some relationships develop slower than others. Some people get impatient quicker than others. But if you feel you'd like to get to know the person better, to hear what their voice sounds like because emails just aren't enough, it's time to talk on the phone. Usually, one person hints that they would like to move away from the dating emails and talk on the phone. They'll give out their phone number, hoping that the other person will give out theirs or at least indicate that they'll call. If your writing partner ignores your hint, or if they never give out a number themselves, this might not be a connection that's going places.

When you do call or your emailer calls you, it doesn't mean that this is a done deal. Not yet. Sometimes that first call lives up to your expectations and you talk for an hour, maybe two. You can't wait to hear from the person again. Sometimes you're disappointed. But you can usually tell after the call if you want to know this person more or not. I suggest that in the first phone call you:

- Don't make it too long unless it feels really easy and fun.
- Stay away from sensitive, divisive topics like politics, sex, religion and race.
- Get a feel for the personality and their core values.

- Find out if they're optimistic or pessimistic, if they have a sense of humor and so on.
- Ask questions about their past that they've mentioned in their profile, because they've already put it out there.
- Don't hog the conversation. Be a good listener.
- Don't end on a sour note if the call isn't going well.
- If the call goes well, you can mention speaking again and see what comes back to you.

Even when the call goes like fireworks, don't get your hopes up. I once had a man I talked to for an hour call me back within an hour to say it was the best call he'd made on that website — and I never heard from him again. But my friend did and we had a good laugh about it. Apparently, he had many best calls!

Infatuation

Beginners are often prone to falling for someone even before they meet them. You see a great looking photograph, the emails seem warm and friendly, and, whoops, there goes your heart. Beware of that! You still don't know the person's character, and you don't even know if there's going to be any chemistry between you.

That wonderful feeling you get when you first meet someone intriguing has a lot to do with your own fantasies, your own hopes and plans for the future. Con artists and scammers love that infatuation reaction because they're easily able to reel you in.

Please, please, please keep your heart in check and wait until you've met the person and get to know him or her well before you fall in love.

Ghosting

Ghosting is when someone disappears from communication. You might be excited about someone, even think there's a real future with them. Then you stop hearing from them. It can be hurtful, even gut wrenching. A word of warning, three sentences, actually:

DO NOT TAKE IT PERSONALLY!

DO NOT PRESSURE THEM!

DO NOT STALK THEM ONLINE!

I've been stalked and it only made me dislike the person more. If you're tempted to pressure someone, talk yourself out of it. They've decided that you're not the right fit for them so give them that freedom. Just blink, breathe — and keep moving. This is not going to be your last opportunity.

The Positive Outcome

After you've spoken to your match a few times on the phone, and you haven't ghosted or been ghosted, it's a good idea to meet. You don't want to drag the online communication out because you might be missing things that you can only see, hear and smell on a person-to-person date.

It's always safest to arrange to meet in a public place where there will be lot of other people. Don't ask to be picked up so that the date knows where you live and NEVER invite your date into your home. I prefer to meet during daylight hours too. A coffee shop or a bar is ideal for a first date because if things are going well, you can stay longer. If they aren't, you can slip away. If you know you're safe, you'll relax and enjoy the date more.

Chapter Eight Checklist

Answer the following, creating your own process, if you plan to meet someone through a dating website.

How much time am I willing to spend every day or week on internet dating?

....

....

Will I actively search for and 'like' people myself, or will I wait until someone 'likes' me?

....

....

How do I check to see if the person I'm communicating with is a scammer or undesirable?

....

....

....

How many emails should I exchange before giving out my phone number?

....

....

Will I wait for the other person to suggest moving to a phone call or will I?

....

....

If I'm disappointed by someone on a phone call or ghosted, how will I react?

....

....

....

Chapter Nine
Going the Matchmaker Route

If you're already groaning about having to go the internet route to find your mate, steady on. There are alternatives, as you will see in the following chapters.

One option is to turn to professionals, and the matchmaking industry has seen a rise in demand for their services from Boomers who prefer face-to-face contact. However — and there are some howevers — I want to be very clear about the positives and negatives in using matchmakers, as well as the do's and don'ts, before you plonk down your money.

I've personally been matched by a professional matchmaker who matched me with three men. She did it for free because I was a challenge to her. Did it go well? Not really. One was so stuck in his rut that he was looking for someone to get down into the rut with him. Another was a narcissist who was focused on his own needs, social and sexual. And the third man didn't have enough money to take me on a date and kept ducking out of getting together.

Nonetheless, others have been successful as we see from the fact that there are currently more than 1,200 matchmaking companies today in the US. Each one offers individualized attention to their customers, from matchmaking and coaching to group events and social gatherings. But you have to engage a matchmaker with the idea that it is still a bit of a crap shoot but you're willing to throw the dice.

So don't give up hope, if you have the time and money, and read the following carefully.

The Fees

You're going to have to take out your wallet for a matchmaking service, because you can end up spending thousands of dollars depending on the company and your needs. Expect to pay a minimum of $7,000 in fees and services at the end of the day because there can be four different fees, some of them hidden.

Initial Consultation Fees: Most matchmaking companies charge an initial fee for assessing your dating preferences, relationship goals and overall compatibility factors.

Membership Packages: You'll need to buy a membership package which can vary in duration and price. These may include a specific number of introductions, coaching sessions and access to social events. This is where you'll have an opportunity to choose exactly what services you need and what price you'll be prepared to pay. And even if you meet someone before you've met all the matches they guarantee you in the package, you will still have to pay the full fee.

Upscale Services: Some companies promise higher-quality matches, background checks and personal attention. Others can arrange dinner with a mixed group of prospective partners. And these services may come with a premium price tag.

Success Fees: In some companies you can be charged an additional fee for a successful match. Read the fine print carefully!

The Upside

I know the fees seem a bit daunting, so why would you sign up for these services? Well, matchmakers tailor their efforts to suit the needs and preferences of each client. And paying those fees gives you a guarantee of safety and security since the company has already vetted your potential matches.

You also get guidance, dating tips and emotional support from your matchmaker along the way, kind of like having a dating therapist. Another advantage is that they have the headache of sorting through the people they have on file to find someone who might be your compatible match, eliminating the need for endless online searches.

This all sounds pretty positive, right? But wait...

The Downside

As with every other option, there are disadvantages to using a matchmaking service. I'm listing and bolding these so you'll have an opportunity to think things through the pros and cons before you pay a dollar.

Financial Investment: Signing up for matchmaking services means making a financial commitment and, for some people, especially those on fixed incomes, the cost can be significant. And once you sign that contract, remember, you have to keep paying, even if you stop using the service.

No Guarantees: Success is not guaranteed, which is what happened in my case. You can invest time and money in these services without finding a match, leading to disappointment.

Fraud: One of the leading matchmaking services just paid out millions to customers who said that they were promised dates who never appeared. In one case, staff from a matchmaking service went on dates with customers just to say that they had had a date. Do your due diligence about matchmaking companies before you decide which one to go with.

Limited Control: Using matchmaking services means giving up some control over your choice of dates. You're going to need to trust their matchmaker's judgment, which can be challenging if you like to make your own decisions.

Limited Pool of Candidates: Matchmaking services depend on their existing database of potential matches. Their pool of candidates is a lot smaller than the online dating pool, which can affect the quality of your matches. Also, you usually sign up and pay for a certain number of matches. Once you've reached that number, game over.

The Emotional Toll: Even if you've invested time, energy and money into a matchmaking service, you can still wind up without a match that sticks. The disappointment can be disheartening and the financial loss can make it seem worse.

The Do's

It's essential to approach a matchmaker with realistic expectations. Here are some pointers to help you.

Do Your Research: Start by researching matchmaking services in your area. Read reviews, ask for recommendations from friends, and make sure that the service has a positive track record with successful matches for seniors like yourself.

Be Honest About Your Expectations: Clearly communicate your relationship goals and expectations with the matchmaking service. Whether you're seeking a friend, a long-term commitment or marriage, you have to be upfront about what you're really looking for.

Be Open-Minded: Stay open to meeting people who don't fit your personal checklist. Sometimes unexpected connections can lead to great relationships. You might meet someone older or younger than you were prepared for, or of a different race, who turns out to be a great partner.

Take Your Time: Don't rush the process. Be patient and allow the matchmaking service to work its magic, even if it takes a bit longer to find the right match.

Engage in Self-Reflection: Think about your past relationships, the good and the bad, to gain insight into what you're really looking for in a partner. After each date, have a frank discussion with your matchmaker to help in this process.

Stay Safe: When meeting potential matches for the first time, choose a public place to meet and tell a friend or family member where you're going and with whom. And always be cautious about sharing your personal information with strangers, even if they've been arranged by your matchmaker.

The Don'ts

Don't Rush Into Anything: Avoid rushing into a relationship too quickly. Take the time to get to know your potential match, and ensure that your connection is built on genuine compatibility.

Don't Compromise on Your Deal Breakers: Your core values and beliefs are vitally important to who you are. Make sure that your potential partner shares your fundamental values.

Don't Judge Solely on Looks: Focus on the person's character, interests and compatibility, not just the pretty face.

Don't Be Discouraged by Rejection: Rejection is part of the dating process, even if your matchmaker is confident that this is a match made in heaven. As we've already said, you have to have a thick skin to look for true love.

Don't Ignore Red Flags: If you notice red flags or have a gut feeling that something isn't right, trust your instincts. Discuss your concerns with the matchmaking service because your safety and well-being should always come first.

Whatever means of meeting a potential mate you choose, you've got to have a positive attitude throughout. Never give up hope!

Chapter Nine Checklist

Dig down deep to answer the following questions.

What are my misgivings about signing up for a matchmaking service?

....

....

Do I have the financial resources to afford such a service?

....

....

Am I ready to give up control in selecting a partner to a matchmaker?

....

....

How will I handle the rejection if I like someone I'm matched with, but they don't want a relationship with me?

....

....

....

Am I willing to attend the social events that the matchmaking service holds? Why?

....

....

How am I going to feel if I have no success with a matchmaking service?

....

....

Would I prefer another way to find a partner? What is it?

....

....

....

....

....

Chapter Ten
Preferring the Serendipitous Meeting

Maybe you're still uncomfortable with the idea of online dating and you've decided not to give your money to matchmaking services. You've asked friends and family members to introduce you to a prospective match but no one of interest has surfaced.

You shrug your shoulders. Fate will step in, you tell yourself. Perhaps you'll meet someone in the library, share a table with them in a coffee shop, or sit beside a good-looking stranger on a train, kind of like the plot of a movie.

What are the Odds?

Unfortunately, those instances are rare, so there might be problems for those waiting for their fairy godmother to step in. An article in the UK's *Daily Mail* in 2023 says the odds of people of any age meeting their mate by chance are one in 562. That's a lot of people to bump into in the supermarket.

The odds will be even higher for seniors, especially women, who greatly outnumber men their own age, and even worse for women of color.

Whatever the race, there's always the issue of a senior sticking to a narrow circle of friends and a limited range of activities. If a man is a golfer, for example, he might spend his spare time with people who golf, most of them partnered already. A woman might stick to her routine, hoping that an eligible stranger will show up in her church one day. Both will probably be disappointed.

The Romance of Coincidence

The idea of meeting someone by chance does hold a certain allure, I know, suggesting a magical (some would even call it spiritual) and unexpected connection. It's as if it were meant to be, right? Fate has brought you together.

There are definitely advantages to meeting someone effortlessly, the old-fashioned way. It's less structured and less expensive than internet dating or matchmaking services, and there's an ease and naturalness to it. When you bump into another person with shared interests or activities, it creates a sense of camaraderie and understanding between you.

The best part about meeting serendipitously is that you can build a connection based on real-life chemistry. It gives you time to observe someone's personality, mannerisms, and nonverbal cues, time you can use to determine if you're both compatible. And since those encounters follow a gradual progression, they create a sense of excitement as the connection deepens.

I totally understand why many of my students say they want to meet someone this way. It's less work, students have said. The problem is that if you stay in your regular routine and rely solely on serendipity, nothing will happen. The only people coming to your front door are the same folks who've always been coming.

How can you increase your chances of meeting a prospective partner the old-fashioned way?

You have to make it happen. The first step is to walk out your front door to meet new people. It takes effort, but it will be worth it. So here are some suggestions to get started.

Pursue interests and hobbies: Engaging in activities and hobbies that genuinely interest you is an excellent way to meet like-minded individuals. Join local clubs, organizations, or community groups centered around your passions. Think about joining a group of people living in your area who share your interests, people of your age, through a Meetup group you can find on www.meetup.com. By doing so, you increase the chances of meeting someone with your interests and values.

Embrace social gatherings: Attend social events, parties and gatherings organized by friends, family or community organizations. If you like the theater and art exhibitions, go regularly to find similarly interested people. I once met a lovely man while both of us were gazing at a painting at an art opening.

Volunteer and give back: Volunteering not only allows you to make a positive impact on your community but also puts you in contact with individuals who share your values. Consider volunteering at local charities, hospitals or community centers.

Explore educational opportunities: Enroll in courses or workshops that genuinely interest you, so don't sign on for anthropology classes if you're going to sleep through them. Take classes that will add to your life. Learning a new language, for example, can improve your travel options. Taking classes will not only help you gain knowledge and improve your cognitive skills, but you'll also have the chance to meet others who share your enthusiasm.

Stay open to new experiences: Embrace spontaneity. Say "yes" to invitations, even if they're outside your comfort zone. You'll increase the likelihood of encountering new and interesting people that way. Anybody for a singles cruise?

Visit new and different places: You can visit different towns and browse the shops, art galleries and restaurants. If you take a history group tour, you could well strike up a friendship with another participant.

Attend unfamiliar churches or spiritual gatherings: If you value spiritual connections, expand the number of churches you visit or take a yoga class if that's your interest. You'll find others of the same mind, making for a deeper connection.

Cultivating the Relationship

Say that you've stepped outside your normal routine and seen someone interesting, what happens next? My advice is not to let it die on the vine. You've got to nurture the connection, and you don't have to wait for the other person to make the first move.

After seeing that fascinating person in a bookstore, for example, start a conversation about a book they're reading. You might discover commonalities that could strengthen the bond between you. Of course, if the other person isn't interested in chatting, remember not to react negatively. It's creepy to have someone stalking you around a bookstore and you don't want to be that person.

If things go well, however, take the initiative and ask for their contact information or suggest meeting for coffee or a casual outing. Taking a proactive approach shows your enthusiasm and makes it clear that you're a confident individual. Also allow the connection to develop naturally. Be patient. Remember that if you're going to build a genuine relationship, it will take time, requiring an understanding of each other's needs and desires.

Let each encounter be an opportunity for growth and connection, regardless of the outcome. Who knows? You might even end up with a great friend or business connection. Nothing ventured, nothing gained, right?

Chapter Ten Checklist

Take a deep breath and think about the questions below.

Do I fantasize about meeting someone by chance? Y/N If yes, what is the fantasy?

....

....

....

....

Am I willing to go outside my regular routine to meet a suitable mate? Why/why not?

....

....

....

....

Is there a group that enjoys a hobby that I do? What is it?

....

....

How do I feel about traveling alone?

....

....

How do I feel about striking up a conversation with a complete stranger?

....

....

....

What volunteer activity could I sign up for that would interest me?

....

....

What events (sports, art, etc.) could I attend that would attract someone who is similarly interested?

....

....

Do I willingly accept social invitations?

....

....

How will I follow up and nurture connections that occur by chance?

....

....

Chapter Eleven
Launching that First Date

A fter going online or meeting someone otherwise, you may now have a date. Congratulations! But it can be intimidating if you haven't gone on a date in years, perhaps even in decades. You feel almost like a teenager the first time around. One student told me that if someone asked her on a date she'd throw up. She didn't. So take a deep breath and keep telling yourself that millions around the world do this, even in their nineties. And you can, too.

Think Ahead

It's best not to make assumptions about the outcome of a first date. Don't get all knotted up thinking that you'll be meeting the love of your life. This is just a date with another human being, regardless of the outcome. Try not to have any expectations. There are many ways in which this first meeting could go well — or go sideways. You could hit it off the first time. Or it could just be one of many dates you chalk up to experience.

I find that first date fascinating. Expect the unexpected is my motto, because I've had a variety of experiences and heard all kinds of stories from other daters. Some people fall in love at first sight. Others want to edge out of the door as soon as they meet. Be prepared for anything. Most of the time the meeting will be fairly uneventful, but occasionally you'll have a date you never forget. There are the dates who turn out to be older or larger than their photographs. There are dates where you might be asked for a loan. One woman I know had a date who requested one of her kidneys!

Even if your date is relatively normal, he or she isn't going to be perfect. They might be as anxious as you. Remind yourself that this is just practice for your future dates.

As I mentioned earlier, a first date should be just a brief meeting in a public place for a snack or a short walk. The time that it takes to drink a cup of coffee is about the length of a date that can be cut short or lengthened as the meeting dictates.

It's important that you let a friend know whom you're meeting and where you're meeting them.

Remember, NEVER give out information about where you live, and definitely don't invite the person to your home, even if you think you trust them. This person is still a stranger to you. You can be raped, held up at gunpoint or worse. Thank goodness, violence is rare in the dating process, but you should always protect yourself.

With your red-flag alert system on high, but preparing for the best, let's get ready for our date.

First Impressions Count

They say it takes five seconds to make a good first impression, so you have to put your best foot forward for your date. That outdated polo shirt with the frayed collar and the moo-moo you wear every day need to stay at home. Slip into an outfit that makes you feel like a million dollars. But don't forget, comfort is key and you don't want to keep worrying about how slim or attractive you look. You can show off your unique style while being comfortable.

Men, do put on a clean, new shirt, save the sandals for another day, and spruce it up with a fresh shave and clean nails. I remember one gentleman who came to meet me with unkempt hair and dirty fingernails. It took less than five seconds to make my decision!

This isn't a dress-up contest but your date will be comparing you with other people — and with the photos you posted. That's why it's important to post recent photographs that look like you today. I'm not the only person who was disappointed that their date was ten years older than their photographs, even of the age they posted.

Authenticity is like catnip for connections, and you want to attract the right folks who'll appreciate you for who you truly are. You don't want to deceive or feel deceived on that big date.

It's not only how you look, however. It's also about smell. Yes, I went there. This might sound unnecessary but believe me, it does happen. Someone goes on a date looking great — but they haven't taken a bath or applied deodorant. That's all your date will remember.

Then there's punctuality. You're looking clean and smelling fresh — but you're late for the date. What impression do you think you'll be making? The answer isn't a good one. It's always best to arrive promptly, even a little before the appointed time, to stake out a table or greet your date. And this goes for males and females. If you get there early, you can calm your anxiety by taking some deep breaths before the person appears.

Make it Easy

When it comes to conversations, keep it natural — yet be yourself. The dialog should flow like a good tennis match, with the ball bouncing back and forth. Equal time. There's nothing more annoying for the listener than a date who hogs the conversation.

Don't be shy to ask questions that show you're interested in getting to know your date better. Chat about their passions, hobbies and what makes them tick. According to the Journal of Experimental Social Psychology, sharing personal stories on a first date sparks a stronger connection and boosts the chances of a second round. So be ready to spill a tale or two.

It's important to be a great listener, too. Give your date your full attention and show that you genuinely want to hear what they're saying. I once had a date with a man who interrupted my description of my family by suddenly saying, "I know why I'm gaining weight. It's the apple juice I've been drinking." He hadn't been listening to a word I was saying. Needless to say, that was our last date.

You can't wait for a second date to make a good first impression. The first date is the interview, often the only one. Increase your chances of success by putting your best foot forward. A dating website, Coffee Meets Bagel, says 70 percent of their users are open to a second date after a successful first one.

Most important of all on that first date is being yourself. Don't try to impress. Don't talk about your expensive car or drop names of important people. That's a definite yawner for others to listen to. Just be genuine, and you'll find that your date will appreciate your realness.

Sex

Occasionally, a date will turn into a wonderful experience and may go on for hours, ending with dinner, dessert and lots of conversation. My advice on those occasions is not to let the situation get into the sexual arena. Wait!

There are several stages to the relationship experience, enough to write another book about. Briefly, I'll say that the first stages are just about getting to know each other. If you want a lasting relationship, you don't want to jump from stage one to stage five in one go. You don't know enough about the person on a first date. You can feel excitement, even get butterflies, but that's just infatuation or maybe lust. You're still a long way away from knowing who you're getting into bed with on a first date.

Some people want to find a date online to have casual sex (no judgement). If you are that person, you need to let your date know what your expectations are before you first meet. But don't end up as a statistic: another senior with a sexually transmitted disease. If you and your date have already discussed the possibility of having sex, and if the date pans out and you go through with it, please wear a condom. If you don't, get tested, especially if it turns out to be a one-night stand.

It can be a shock for someone looking for a lasting, deep connection to discover that their date is just looking for a casual relationship. That's why I recommend a phone call to sound the other person out about what they're looking for in a mate.

When the Date Ends

Towards the end of the date, if you think things have been going well, let your date know. If you're not interested in continuing the relationship, just thank them for meeting you and end on a cheerful note. No promises, no plans. Of course, if things went swimmingly, the second date will be planned naturally.

Then there's the age-old question of who pays the bill. It's not as tricky as you might think. If you initiated the date, it's a sweet gesture to offer to foot the bill. But if your date insists on sharing the cost or treating you, accept it graciously. It's all about showing respect and keeping things balanced. No need for a tug-of-war; just keep it easygoing.

When you part, there's no written rule about whether to hug or not, whether to kiss on the cheek or pat the other's arm. Just do what feels appropriate. A terrible date might mean a smile and speedy departure. A great date might end in a hug, but I wouldn't kiss someone on that first date without asking their permission. It's all about being respectful.

Even if you don't plan to meet the person again, you might encounter them somewhere down life's road. That's happened to more than one person I know. So keep the end of the date friendly and kind, no matter what.

After the Date

Whether your meeting went well or not, you may want to write a follow-up note to thank the other person for making time and effort to meet with you. If things went well, you might politely mention that another date would be welcome. If you don't want another date, don't mention it but wish the person well in finding love. Even if you write and the other person doesn't reciprocate, accept that you were not what they were looking for and carry on to the next date.

Not every first date will turn into a Hollywood romance, and that's just life. But stay positive. Every date is a chance to learn, grow, and figure out what you're looking for. I tell my students to think of every date as practice for the next. Remember the old frog story about doling out a few kisses before you find your prince or princess.

I'm going to end this chapter with some solid advice from another dating coach: date more than one person at the same time until you find that special someone. You won't focus so intently on that one date that you become too emotionally involved. Keep playing the field until you're sure about your choice and you both agree to be exclusive. Then you can let your emotions soar!

Chapter Eleven Checklist

Are you ready to go on a date? Answer these questions before you meet your prospective partner.

Do I usually make assumptions before meeting someone? If so, what are they?

....

....

Have I checked the person's background using a reliable website to do so?

....

....

How will I overcome any nervousness?

....

....

What topics will I discuss with my date?

....

....

....

....

When it comes to paying the check, what will I do?

...............…..

...............…..

How will I react if my date doesn't invite me on a second date?

...............…..

...............…..

Am I open to dating more than one person at a time?

...............…..

...............…..

...............…..

...............…..

...............…..

Chapter Twelve
Going Your Own Way

You might be all excited about getting your dating process started, might have even had a couple dates by the time you read this chapter.

Needless to say, however, dating isn't for every senior single. After reading this book, you may decide that you'd just rather not go to the trouble of looking for a mate. You might even prefer what you have right now and choose not to change anything. Focusing on your work, your current life, your family or those close to you might be enough.

There's no shame to wanting to go it alone if you decide that you don't want to be in an emotionally intimate relationship, and you have several living choices to achieve that.

Embracing Solitude

You might decide that you'd rather live alone. Maybe you've decided that being alone allows you to make decisions freely, set your own routine and create a space that reflects your personality, without having to consider the needs or imposition of a partner.

There are several advantages to living alone. The most important one, of course, it that it can provide us with the freedom to live life on our own terms, making decisions without external influence. Like some of you, I love having my own space and quiet sometimes. There's time for my writing, as well as introspection and personal growth. But I do like company, so living entirely alone may not be right for me.

Those who choose to have no roommate or partner often relish the complete privacy and freedom to maintain their own schedule. They feel at their best when they can manage a household independently, maybe with some help cleaning as they get older, but being in complete control of their environment suits their lifestyle. I get it.

There are, however, drawbacks to permanent aloneness. For some seniors, living alone can lead to feelings of isolation and loneliness, especially if they lack a strong social support network. It can result in poorer mental and physical health, as reported by numerous researchers.

If you have an accident or suddenly fall ill, will you have the ability to reach out and call someone? When you feel lonely, do you have easy access to socializing? There are also the household chores and responsibilities and, of course, the increased financial strain, with no partner or roommate to share expenses.

People who live alone have to weigh their desire for solitude against their very real financial, physical and emotional needs. It will become vitally important to have an emergency plan, like an arrangement with neighbors to check on them every day to make sure they're okay, or having a medical alert necklace or bracelet to call 911 if they fall. Planning ahead for any eventuality becomes really essential when one lives alone.

Thriving in Community

If living alone isn't for you, there's always the option of living with others. I have personally considered moving in with friends as I age, rather like *The Golden Girls*. Thanks to that TV series as well as our economic times, community living options for seniors have soared in popularity. Unlike the days of hippie communes, seniors can now choose from various living arrangements, including living in group homes with friends, sometimes called co-housing. They can also live in co-ops with like-minded individuals who share similar interests and values.

There are lots of advantages to co-habitation. It fosters social interaction, reducing feelings of isolation and promoting a sense of belonging. Seniors in a community can pool resources, which may lead to cost savings and shared responsibilities. Many community setups offer security features and on-site support staff, ensuring seniors' safety and well-being. The best part is that there are group activities, outings and events, promoting a socially active lifestyle.

There are always pros and cons to any lifestyle. Living in a community may mean sacrificing some level of privacy compared to living alone. You will be living in close proximity with others, and might experience occasional conflicts or differences in opinion. Tempers might flare as personalities clash. And occasionally, depending on the community, the costs associated with communal living can be higher than living alone.

Living with Family

Living with family is a more traditional choice for single seniors, especially if they have a close relationship with their adult children or other relatives.

Family life can provide seniors with emotional support, companionship and a strong sense of family bonding. Of course, combining households can result in financial savings, easing the burden of expenses for both seniors and their family members. You can share household chores and responsibilities, reducing the workload for everyone.

On the other hand, living with family may require compromise to accommodate the needs and preferences of

106

others. You may need to adjust to sharing living spaces and respecting others' boundaries. What happens when Grandpa objects to a teenager's outfit? With all the emotions associated with family, things can get heated!

My advice to people moving in with family is to create boundaries early, since familiarity can breed contempt. Ground rules should be outlined, in writing if necessary, about when and how people can enter your space, how much you will be contributing to the expenses and other details. I'd even suggest these should be ironed out before you move in to save on the arguments and the stress.

It's Up to You

You are the only person who can decide what is right for you going forward, a choice not influenced by others or the media. You have to consider your own personal preferences, financial situation, and social support network. Each choice, living with a loved one, living alone, living in a community or with family, comes with its unique set of possibilities, advantages and disadvantages. Ultimately, the key to your living arrangement lies in embracing what aligns with your lifestyle, values and future plans.

Whether it's having a partner or choosing to have independence, thriving in a social community or living with family, you now have the opportunity to create a living arrangement that brings you joy in your new chapter of life.

Dating is now a very real option for you to contemplate in that new chapter. Even the supreme TV dater, *The Bachelor*, is now a Boomer. The subject of multiple conversations, programs, articles and books, senior dating is happening all around us. You can choose to participate in dating or stay away from it. You can date only when you want some company, making sure you are safe and secure. You might decide to postpone the idea of dating for the time being, or you may know deep within you that it's not right for you. Just make sure your decision is in your own best interest. It's all up to you.

I wish you good health, happiness and peace of mind on whatever path you choose, my friend.

Chapter Twelve Checklist

Write out your thoughts about your own living and relationship choices going forwards.

....

....

....

....

....

....

....

....

....

....

....

....

....

....

....

....

....

....

....

....

....

The beginning…

THIRD ACT DATING

A GUIDE TO COMPANIONSHIP FOR SILVER SINGLES

Visit us online at:
www.ThirdActDating.com

Printed in Great Britain
by Amazon

37409254R00071